SPIRITUAL BLOOMING

BELINDA CALDERON

PAGE PUBLISHING, INC.
New York, NY

First originally published by Page Publishing, Inc. 2019

ISBN 978-1-64584-800-4 (Paperback)
ISBN 978-1-64584-801-1 (Digital)

Printed in the United States of America

CONTENTS

Summary...5

Chapter 1: The Cursed Blood.................................7
Chapter 2: Black One, Bad One 9
Chapter 3: Protection 11
Chapter 4: True Blood 13
Chapter 5: Enlightenment Kingdom....................16
Chapter 6: Vlalore 19
Chapter 7: The Curse 21
Chapter 8: Master Sahib, Lost City.....................23
Chapter 9: Chakras...25
Chapter 10: Home..30
Chapter 11: Princess Coronation 33
Chapter 12: Sachi 38
Chapter 13: The Tree of Life................................41
Chapter 14: The Truth..44
Chapter 15: Last Part...48
Chapter 16: The True Me 52
Chapter 17: Elemental Kingdom 55
Chapter 18: My Other Half...................................61
Chapter 19: Sacrifice..66
Chapter 20: The End of the Beginning..................69

SUMMARY

A child will be born as the Sachi. This child's powers will be greater than any. This child will save us all from our destiny. The child will be born in the Enlightenment Kingdom. The child will be named. The future we see shall be for now until this child is born. As we come to terms of this mess this world has created for us, we must push back this madness and keep going forward. Until then, this world will have to wait for its savior.

Chapter 1

THE CURSED BLOOD

"Uhhhh!" Screaming could be heard throughout the whole universe.

"Come on, Egjyll, I need you to push again, Egjyll, push hard."

"Luke, please hold my hand."

Luke was her lover, friend, and now husband. Egjyll pushed with all her strength and stopped; baby's screams could be heard.

"It's a girl," the doctor said, wrapping the blanket around the baby girl.

The doctor then gave the baby to Egjyll. The couple was so happy and then sad at the same time.

"What's her name?" asked the doctor and nurses who wanted to know.

"Her name is Haven," Luke said as he took his baby girl from his wife's hands to hold her for the first and last time.

Luke walked to the window with Haven in his hands and looked into her beautiful blue-red eyes. "My baby girl, one day you will love someone like me and your mother do." Luke's tears started to drop. "Please break this curse, for I will no longer live to see you walk, grow, or even give you away on that special day I love you, my little princess Haven." Luke kissed the baby goodbye, handing her back to Egjyll. He kissed Egjyll one last time. "Egjyll, one day when she is ready, please tell her of our tale, me and who she really is, I love you both."

The ground began to shake; the doctor looked to the couple.

"Luke, are you ready?"

Luke nodded his head and looked back at Egjyll with a look of sadness in his eyes, then walked on forward with the doctor to another room. Soon everything stopped, and there lay Egjyll crying with her baby in her hands.

"Haven, I will always protect you and never tell you about any of this, for this secret and curse is for me to keep alone."

Chapter 2

BLACK ONE, BAD ONE

rip, drip, splash!

Once again, another rainy day. Does this place ever stop raining? It's like every time I feel sad or gloomy, it starts to rain. Walking in this cold, wet weather getting all my clothes wet, Mom works so hard to keep these clean and neat for me. My mother is a single parent, and I am her only child I wish I could say I were like any other kid, but I'm not, I am different.

Walking in the entrance to my school, by now all my clothes are wet. As I walk past all the kids, they just stare at me, saying, "Man, look at her, she tries too hard, that slut! She's good for nothing but making trouble."

I just keep walking until I reach my locker. Putting my stuff inside, when I close my locker, I look over to my right, and there she is Avisha Chess. She has the most beautiful green eyes, and her hair is a brownish color, long and wavy. She walks past me every day and just smiles, even sometimes waves at me. I just turn around like I don't know her, which I do, but who would talk to a weird person.

The bell has rung for first period. I wait a little until everybody is gone and stood there in the middle of the hall, and that's when they appear—the spirits of all sorts and shapes, walking past me like I also didn't exist. But there stands one, a black one. I can feel his bad aura. His eyes are a red color. They stare into my very soul. Deep inside, I can feel him wanting to tear me from the inside out. I fear these things. I tell my mom, and she doesn't say anything, but her boyfriend always calls me crazy.

The black one is now coming straight at me; he moves quicker than the other spirits. The spirits disappear in fear of him, and then there it is and me face-to-face, staring as if our very lives depended on it.

"If spirits threaten me in this place, fight water by water and fire by fire, banish their souls into nothingness, and remove their powers until the last trace. Let these evil beings flee, through time and space."

A ball of shining light comes at us. I jump out of the way to avoid it. The black one turns around and is hit by the strong ball of light, disappearing. I look up from where this ball of light comes from. There she stands, Avisha Chess.

"Are you okay?" she says while running toward me, helping me up from the floor.

I just nod my head.

"Well, next time, Haven, you should be more careful, these things can kill you if you're just being a bystander."

The only thing I am worried about is that the most popular girl in school knows my name.

"I better be going then." She heads right back to her class and me to mine.

The day has gone by fast, and it is time to head home.

Chapter 3

PROTECTION

Rainy, cloudy gray clouds still loom over the sky as the wind blows hard. Rain comes down harder than it has done this morning. I still walk in the rain with no umbrella to cover me. My home is three blocks away from school. Crow Street is where I live, in the very house everyone fears and think to be cursed. The grass is always gloomy; no living thing is alive. The front of the house looks like no one lives there. As I step closer to the door, I reach for the knob and turn.

Screaming can be heard and things breaking. I run in to find my mother on the ground in the kitchen with him standing over her with a beer in his hand and a smoke in the other. He looks my way as I stand there in shock; he turns back to my mom and starts kicking her. I am too shocked to move or to do something, until something comes over me, and I bolt from the ground. I ran toward him, knocking him to the ground, the beer bottle breaking. I run over to my mom and check her.

"Mom, are you okay?"

She just shakes her head yes. I help her get up when I am tackled to the ground, and I feel a heavy body on top of me holding my collar.

The next thing hits me hard in the eye. I can feel myself fading away, and everything becomes blurry. I hear my mom yelling something like, "Don't grab that broken beer bottle."

That's when I feel a sting on my upper arm; I feel the weight being lifted off me. I sit up as the blurriness goes away, and I look around to find my mother next to me, helping me up, and there he stands proud and bold.

"Next time, little girl, you won't be so lucky," Mike says as my mother leads me out of the room, up the stairs to my room.

My mother insists on helping me, but I don't let her. I head into my room on my own and just lie on the bed in pain. I look out the window as the sun shines on me through the window, and then I look back at the ceiling, wondering when my life begin will.

"Oh, God, if you can hear me know, please save me." I sigh and wrap my arm up and put on a tank top on and lie in bed as the darkness takes over.

The next day is a pain. I leave my tank top on, and I just put on a zip-up jacket, pulling the hood over to cover my black eye. I am at my locker, avoiding everyone today, even the spirits, but then again, no one notices I am here except her, Avisha. I feel her presence next to me

"Haven, are you all right? You're dressed different, and you've been out of it the whole day."

Everyone has cleared out, and it is just me and her. I close my locker, walking away from it, when she grabs me by the upper arm where he has cut me.

"Uhhhh!" I scream, holding on to the wound.

"Haven, I am sorry, I didn't mean to." My hood has fallen. "Haven, what happened to your eye?"

That's when I wanted to run away, but then I am pulled into a hug. "Don't move. He is here."

I want to know who, so I speak for the first time, "Who?" I turn around, and there he stands, the guy who has given me the cut and a black eye. He is the black one.

Chapter 4

TRUE BLOOD

Mike is the black shadow we saw the other day. But why is he here?

"Haven, he is here to finish the job to kill you."

I have tears coming down my eyes, and I want to get out of here and run home to my mom. I look at Avisha, and she looks at me.

"Don't worry, Haven, I will always protect you, be by your side."

I haven't heard those word said to me at all. Looking back at Mike, he is now running toward us at full speed.

"Haven, we need to get you home now, we need to talk to your mother."

I just nod my head, and we leave the school, heading toward my home where my mother will be. Crow Street is now in view, and there is my house. As we got closer, black shadows like Mike appear but are smaller.

Avisha throws lights of balls at every one of them, making a path for us to get through. We burst through the door, and there she stands, startled, turning around with a look on her face.

"Princess Avisha."

Avisha just looks at her and says, "She needs to go now. She's in too much danger. Her mother needs to know that she needs to know now."

My mother grabs something from underneath the kitchen sink, and a portal opens.

"Thank you, Nina. Be safe." Avisha looks at me. "Haven, everything will be explained, but do not let go of my hand, but if we do get separated, tell them you are looking for Egjyll and that I sent you."

I just nod my head when the door opens, and there stands Mike. Avisha pushes up through the portal. I hold on to her for a while when I feel myself slipping and we are separating.

The next thing I know is that the ground is only a few feet away and *splat* is all you hear. I try to get up, but a weight is on top of me. When I hear doors open and I see green shoes, I turn around and look up at this beautiful woman with blue eyes, blond hair with a golden crown, and a long, green, wavy dress.

"What is your purpose, human?" this woman speaks.

"The queen speaks to you," the soldier-like man says next to me as he hits me on the head.

Before being knocked out, I say one word, "Egjyll." As I lie back on the floor, I hear her say "Haven." The darkness takes over me.

"Haven, Haven dear, you need to get up, honey, you need to wake up. You need to know something. I need to tell you something."

I open my eyes. I look up to the sky and see blue everywhere. The last thing I remember is going through a portal that led me here, meeting this woman, and when I have said "Egjyll," the last thing I hear is her saying my name and the darkness has taken over.

I sit up and look around me. There is yellowish corn field around me; it looks more wheat. It is very beautiful sight to see. I stand up and look around for the source of voice I have heard earlier. I look in front of me, and in the distance, I see a man standing there, a man I don't recognized. This man looks at me, waving his hand as if he wanted me to come over.

I am just staring at him like "What is he saying?" But my insists take over. I walk toward this man. As I got closer to him, he tells me to stop, but I just keep on going. I then bump into a glass wall, realizing it is a barrier separating us.

He says, "Haven."

I look up at him. He looks so familiar as an image appears in my head. Why does he look so familiar?

"Haven, my dear daughter." I look around, as if he were making a mistake. My name is Haven, but when I look at him, he smiles. He can't be, but why is he here?

"Haven dear, my dearest daughter, you have to know about this curse. You have to break this curse."

I give him a look like "What are you talking about?"

"You're my father?" I just have so many questions.

"My dear Haven, you must break the curse," he says this repeatedly.

I don't understand him. "What curse? How do I even break it?"

"Ask the one called Queen of the Enlightenment World to break this curse, or you and I shall never live again. Please break this curse and set me free."

He begins to fade away. I feel tears starting to form in my eyes. I get closer to the glass, wanting to hold on to him.

"Haven, my princess, don't cry, for you are the key to everything. I shall be with you on your journey and guide you."

He turns around and looks back at me with a scared face. All of a sudden, I see someone walking toward him. He puts his hand on the glass, and I read his lips. "I love you." The darkness takes over his side, coming toward him. He says one last thing, "If I don't go, they will find you, and save us all." He walks toward the darkness and disappears. Then the darkness takes over me again as I feel my body hit the ground.

Chapter 5

ENLIGHTENMENT KINGDOM

Time is…
Too slow for those who wait,
Too swift for those who fear,
Too long for those who grieve,
Too short for those who rejoice,
But for those who love,
Time is eternal.

I can feel myself repeating that in my head. As soon as I feel something sharp hit my skin, I jump and scream, opening my eyes. I see the glass windows broken and what looks like a maid holding her ears. Then she lets her hands down.

"You're awake, good, I will get the—"

Before she could finish, I grab her hand and ask, "Where am I?"

She looks at me with a worried look. "You are at the Enlightenment Kingdom where people can connect with the dead along with other powers."

I let go of the maid's hand, and she bows to this man standing at the door.

"Sandra, please fetch Her Majesty." The maid nods.

This man then walks over to me and pulls up a chair. "So are you going to tell me what was that you said just a minute ago, or am I going to have to squeeze it out of you? How do you know our say-

16

ing?" He grabs on to my hand and squeezes hard, hurting me, staring into my very soul just like Mike did.

"Jaffar, you are need downstairs."

He turns his head. I look around him and see the very same woman when I have first come here. Jaffar turns back around and gives me an evil look, lets go of my arm, and walks out as the maid follows. Jaffar and the lady at the door just stare at each other. Then Jaffar leaves with the maid behind him, leaving me and the lady alone.

The lady walks over to the window and just stares at it. "You must leave, Haven, you don't belong here."

I just stare at her and spoke, "I have nowhere to go. I was chased out of my home." I look down, ready to cry.

"Haven, you were never meant to be here with us, you have three days, and begone." She turns toward the door and walks out, leaving me there in thought.

Morning comes, and it is the first day of my three days. I wake up really early. I am about to get up from the bed when Sandra the maid walks in.

"Good morning, milady, here are your clothes. The queen said you may explore whatever you like." She leaves, leaving the clothes on the chair.

I get dressed and head toward the door, poking my head out looking from side to side to find nobody there. The other maids just look at me when I look ahead of me, and there stands a beautiful door with vines and greens all over it, leading into what looks to be a garden.

Putting my hand on the knob and twisting it, I open it to find a beautiful garden with birds chirping and trees moving as well as vines. This garden is alive. As I step in further, I could feel this weird energy, as if something were pulling me. I hear the wind singing and pushing me toward this big tree in the middle of the garden. As I get closer, I feel the energy get more stronger, and then I stop right in front of the tree.

"Haaavvveeennn," I hear my name being called. I look around to find no one. I look back to the tree to find its branches moving. "Haven."

I touch the tree, but before I could, I hear my name from the lady again. "Haven, no," and a vision comes up: a woman in a hospital bed with a beautiful baby girl and a man walking away with the doctor, then the vision goes to a bright light, and I can feel power raging through me and hear a voice. "You will be the savior, and break this curse, Haven my dear."

I am brought back to reality, still feeling the power inside me. I let go of the tree and fall to the ground on my knees. Egjyll is there in seconds, and as I look up to her face, I can see concern all over her face.

"Haven, are you okay? Come and sit."

I do as she says, and I look back at her and say, "It was you in that hospital, and that man walking away was my father." She looks at me and turns away. "Haven, you must leave, you can't stay here for long, they will find you and kill you, or worse take you away from me, you must return to the human world."

I look back at her. "I can't. This guy named Mike came after me on my eighteenth birthday, and if it wasn't for Avisha Chess, I wouldn't be alive now."

Egjyll looks as Haven with surprise and then relief. "I have no choice but to tell you tomorrow in the library, the main one, meet me there, and I will tell you everything you need to know."

With that being said, I go straight to bed thinking about tomorrow. Finally all my questions will be answered.

Chapter 6

VLALORE

Morning comes. Sandra the maid leaves me with clothes for me to get dress in. A couple of minutes later, someone else walks in my room.

"Well, well, what do we have here, another toy for me to play with."

I turn around and scream and start throwing things at him.

My mother runs in. "Vlalore, what are you doing in here? Get out now before I get your mother." She pushes him out and closes the door behind her.

A few minutes later, I finish dressing and head downstairs to the dining hall to find everybody there and the perv guy. Sandra the maid sits me down next to him.

"So what's your name, sweet thing?"

I ignore him. "I don't give my name to those who are nonrespectful to women."

All of a sudden everyone rises except me, and there stands someone I don't recognize. She walks toward me. "Show some respect, you filthy human."

Before she can do anything, my mother stands in front of her. "This child you will not touch. She is my daughter. You need to show some respect to your future leader."

Everybody is on their knees, bowing to me, except the other woman.

"Apzohra!" As my mother screams, she then bows to me. "I am sorry, Egjyll. I didn't know you had a daughter."

Everybody sits back in their seats; everybody has moved away from me, even Vlalore scoots away. Breakfast is quiet. After everybody is done, I am the first to leave.

"Haven, wait."

I don't turn around to see who followed me. I don't care. I run all the way to the outside of the castle and fall to my knees crying in the middle of the front yard.

"Stupid, stupid girl crying."

I look up, and there he stands, Mike.

"Mmmm, I can smell your blood now. It smells just your mother, and her blood can break this curse. All you have to do is come with me, and all will be well." He holds his hand out.

"Haven, don't go with him, come with me, and I will set you free. I know you're scared of losing the people you love and you're afraid people might not love you for you." I look at the person behind me, and it is him, Vlalore. "Please take my hand, let's figure this out together."

I reach for his hand; sparks flow through my body like fireworks going off. He pulls me up, and then his hand burns and he lets go.

"You stupid boy, only true love can break this curse. You touch her, and you could die or live. She can't control her true powers." I look back at Vlalore and see my mother coming; I turn to see Mike gone. She runs toward me and hugs me. "Haven, are you okay?"

I see Vlalore's mother hug him and say, "You need to stay away from her. She can kill you."

I hug my mom tighter, and then she says, "Haven, let's go to the library, you need to know about the curse and everything." She grabs my hand, leading me to big, brown doors, and she opens them to a huge library with lots of books. "Haven, this is where all your answers will be answered." She looks back at me and smiles. "Your father would be proud of you, my baby."

I feel tears coming down. "Mom."

She starts crying. "So let's get started."

Chapter 7

THE CURSE

She holds out her hands. "Haven, please sit."

Mom starts walking back and forth, thinking out loud, "This is hard for me. I don't even know where to start." She is staring straight at me. "It all started with your ancestors a long time ago, the witches and wizards decide to pair each of us with that one person whom we were supposed to love a long time, no rules except a gifted must never fall in love with a witch or wizard until one of your ancestors did, Edzax Enlightenment, who fell in love with a witch named Hope Awakening. Their love was forbidden. Hope was a famous witch, and Edzax was future king to the Enlightenment Kingdom. One day Hope had found her other half, Marcus, and Edzax had an arranged marriage. Soon Hope had rejected Marcus, who didn't really love her, he was using her for power. Edzax had done the same. Edzax and Hope met in secret and soon fell in love, until one day the high witches and wizards had found out about their forbidden love and placed a curse on them both that's never meant to be broken."

I get up and walk around thinking, not understanding her.

Pacing back and forth with my hand on my hip, I ask, "So, Egjyll, what was the curse?"

She looks at me, sighing. "The curse is, when a descendant of the Enlightenment Kingdom family member falls in love with a wizard or a witch, they must die in fourteen days, which is two weeks to stop the earth and humanity from disappearing. There is no way to break this curse, but some have said there is, and yet no one has done it. Breaking the curse comes with a price, humanity must disappear, but the earth remains."

I stop pacing and now stand in front of my birth mother. "Is this what happened to my father?"

She looks at me. "Yes, this is what happened to your father. He sacrificed himself for us and humanity. He always believed that you were destined to break this curse and save us all."

I look at all the books in the library and says, "Mom, I bet there is something in here that can break the curse."

I start searching around, looking at every title of the book.

"Haven, you won't find anything in the books. I searched already. You might as well as give up."

I stop and look to my mother. "I will never be a quitter, this has to be my destiny to save us all, the gift must know that's there is still hope out there, and I will be that hope, no more running away or hiding. It's time to face our fears and fight for what is ours."

My mother now stands in front of me. "There is someone who can help. There is a tree that stands in middle of the forest. That's where the answers you seek will be answered."

I go over and hug my mom that I barely know. "Thank you."

She hugs me tighter. "But first you must learn how to control your powers as well as discover them."

Chapter 8

MASTER SAHIB, LOST CITY

Three days later, Egjyll takes my hand, leading me through a maze of bushes to a wide-open space, with what looks like ancient markings. She lets go of my hand and starts whistling like a bird. Soon thousands of doves appear, and a man appears.

"Egjyll my dear, what have you called me for now?"

She runs up to him, bowing to him. "This is my daughter, Haven."

He looks at me, walking straight to me.

"She—"

Before Mom can finish, he says, "This girl is a true gifted." My mother looks at this man with a surprised face. "She doesn't get her blood from you, maybe her father." The man turns around, and they both start talking.

"Excuse me, but what does that mean?"

Egjyll looks back at me as well as the man does.

Mom starts speaking, "A true gifted is a person who possesses the blood of an ancient city lost long ago. This city we stand in is their home, your home."

I look around and see what my mom is talking about; old ancient buildings stand as the vines and grass cover it from the world seeing it.

I then look back at them, and my mom says something I have never heard her say, "You can break this curse."

All of sudden, a gust of wind spins around me. I keep my ground from falling. Within the wind a whisper can be heard, "You found it, my dear, fulfill your destiny." The wind then dies down.

My mother then looks from the man and then me. "Master."

He looks at my mom and nods. "Egjyll, it's time for you to leave. I will teach her all she needs to know about herself and her history."

My mom runs over to me and hugs me. "Haven, my dear, learn well, these worlds need you." She runs back where we've come from, and everything disappears. All there left standing is me and the man.

"Haven, you will address me by Master Sahib, and your new name will be Sachi, the blessed child." He walks toward me. "This is where the battle was held, shall we see what you have?" He stands in a fight stance. "Dragon breath."

Fire starts coming out of his mouth, heading toward me. I try and dodge it but get burned a little; he does this over and over, and each time I get burned.

"Come on, Sachi, show me what you got."

He does the dragon breath again, but this time I go faster, and I am right behind him, about to kick him, when he stops my kick with one hand. "Good job, Sachi." He lets go of my foot and walks off while saying, "We start your real training tomorrow."

With that said, I go to bed, awaiting a journey ahead of me.

Chapter 9

CHAKRAS

"Run, run, run, run faster, faster, tornado spin." A huge sandstorm in a form of a tornado circles around my master.

I am now twenty, and it has been three years since I started my training. I just must learn about my chakras, which can give me more power. The ancient blood that runs through me belongs to my father's side, along with the gifted and witch and wizard blood. They call me the blessed one, Sachi.

I stand there with my huge sandstorm, ready to make my next move.

"Oh, Sachi, is that all you got?" Soon my sand tornado is swooped away with one hand. Master is now walking toward me. "Dragon breath of fury."

I put my hands together and my feet together and think of the ground growing. "Giant wall of stone." Soon the stone wall comes up, and I try and hold it with my two hands, but I always lose control. Soon I can feel my eyes changing colors to an icy blue. He soon runs to the side of me while I hold my stone wall up. I put too much energy into my stone wall; it's too hard for me to put it down.

I see him smiling. "Dragon breath of extreme fury."

That's the worst fury ever; it can kill me. I have to think fast. "Dragon frost breath." Two elements that are opposite of each other can help, but I have something up my sleeve. My frost breath is pushing his fire breath back. I can see his face is like, "How she is doing that?" I let go of the regular breath and say, "Thunder, frost breath of extreme." I push his fire breath back, and then a big explosion goes off.

I stand my ground and see him do the same, only to find a bunch of burned spot all over him. He smiles. "Well done, Sachi, you have certainly surpassed me." He stands straight, puts his hands together, and bows to me. He stands up and smiles at me. "Sachi, it's time you learn to control your chakras, which will help you control your greatest power, Ajal and Vivi."

He points his hand to the ground to sit. I do as he says.

"Now, Haven, Sachi, listen carefully. Your first chakra, the root chakra, is the first chakra and is located at the base of the spine. It is the root of your being and establishes the deepest connections with your physical body, your environment, and with the earth.

"Muladhara is the most instinctual of all chakras—it is your survival center. Your fight-and-flight response is initiated from this chakra. This is your primal, animal nature. The energy of Muladhara allows us to harness courage, resourcefulness, and the will to live during trying times. It connects us with spiritual energies of our ancestors, their challenges and their triumphs.

"Since base chakra carries our ancestral memories, basically everyone experiences challenges or blockages within Muladhara. War, famine, natural disasters, and any events that threaten our basic survival are all recorded within energies of the first chakra. These memories are imprinted in the subtle body and are passed down from generation to generation, creating unconscious generational patterns.

"It is our work to take responsibility for our own lives and bring to light that which is unconscious. All the seven chakras are import- ant and interconnected with each other. Usually, balancing one chakra will create change in another chakra. It is important, though, to balance the root chakra first, before we proceed to others, or we will lack the stability and rootedness necessary for true transforma- tion and personal growth. We cannot grow and change unless we feel safe and secure. Have you got that down, Sachi?"

I nod my head yes.

"Good, now the second chakra is the sacral chakra, it is your passion and pleasure center, and it is in the pelvic area. While the root chakra is satisfied with survival, the second chakra seeks pleasure and enjoyment. The gift of this chakra is experiencing our lives through feelings and sensations.

"The second chakra is the center of feeling, emotion, pleasure, sensuality, intimacy, and connection. The energy of this chakra allows you to let go, to move, and to feel change and transformation occurring within your body. It allows you to experience this moment as it is, in its own fullness.

"The main challenge for the second chakra is the conditioning of our society. We live in a society where feelings are not valued, where passion and emotional reactions are being frowned upon. We are being taught not to 'lose control.' And we get disconnected from our bodies, our feelings.

"As if this was not enough, we also experience the wounds of our collective cultural struggles over many sexual issues of our society. On one hand, sexuality is magnified and glorified, and on the other hand, it is rejected. This results in either blocked or excessive second-chakra issues. No wonder we have so many issues with our passion center, the wellspring of feelings, enjoyment, and sensuality.

"Do you love your body? Do you enjoy feeling your body? When was the last time you walked barefoot on the grass and felt the sensation of ground underneath your feet?

"The sacral chakra is also your center of creativity. Passion is the fuel of creative energy. Everything you create, a poem, a drawing, or a website, originates from the energy of second chakra. It is also where your fertility originates. After all, conceiving a child is a creative process. A person with an open Svadhisthana chakra is passionate, present in her body, sensual, creative, and connected to her feeling.

"Got it? Good. Moving on now, the third chakra is the solar plexus chakra, located between the navel and solar plexus, it is the core of our personality, our identity, of our ego.

"The third chakra is the center of willpower. While the sacral chakra seeks pleasure and enjoyment, the third chakra is all about the perception of who you are. The gift of this chakra is sensing your personal power, being confident, responsible, and reliable.

"The third chakra is the center of your self-esteem, your will-power, self-discipline, as well as warmth in your personality. The energy of this chakra allows you to transform inertia into action and movement. It allows you to meet challenges and move forward in your life. The main challenge for the third chakra is to use your personal power in a balanced manner. What does that mean? It means consciously harnessing the energy of the solar plexus chakra. It means being proactive rather than reactive or inactive.

"Beings with excessive third chakra energy react to life circumstances, they have emotional outbursts and are often stressed out. Beings with blocked or deficient third chakra are passive and inactive, allowing life to pass by while they do nothing.

"Strong third chakra reflects the ability to move forward in life with confidence and power. It reflects the ability to make conscious choices to choose and to act. The message of the third chakra is, 'You have the power to choose.' You can choose to achieve your life purpose, or you can live out your karma or past experiences.

"What do you choose? Do you choose love, light, and healing? Do you accept that you have the power to choose? Do you feel a sense of freedom when you make a choice? The third chakra is the center of your self-esteem. Every time you judge or criticize yourself, you deplete this chakra and weaken your willpower. Self-love, self-acceptance, and acknowledgement of your own worth are the building blocks of the third chakra.

"A woman with an open and balanced Manipura chakra values herself and her work, is confident in her ability to do something well, loves and accepts herself, is willing to express herself in a powerful way, knows that she has the freedom to choose to be herself and direct her own life.

"That's all the chakras I will teach you besides this one you really need to know, it's called the third eye chakra, and transcends time. It is located in the brain, at the brow, above the base of the nose.

"The gift of this chakra is seeing, both inner and outer worlds. The energy of this chakra allows us to experience clear thought as well as gifts of spiritual contemplation and self-reflection. Through the gift of seeing, we can internalize the outer world, and with symbolic language, we can externalize the inner world.

"The energy of Anja allows us to access our inner guidance that comes from the depths of our being. It allows us to cut through illusion and to access deeper truths—to see beyond the mind, beyond the words. The 'way of the third eye' is seeing everything as it is from a point of 'witness' or 'observer,' or from simply being mindful—moment by moment.

"It means examining self-limiting ideas and developing wisdom that comes from a perspective that transcends the duality of good or bad, black or white. It means seeing and helping others to see the deeper meanings of the situations in their lives.

"Sixth chakra is holistic in nature. When this chakra is fully activated, both hemispheres of the brain function in synchrony. The right hemisphere's creativity and synthetic thinking is integrated and balanced with left hemisphere's logical and analytical thinking.

"The third eye is not only the seat of wisdom but also a seat of conscience. This is where you not only see what is going on but you also know what it means. This is where your sense of justice and your ethics originate. When your third eye is open, you not only see, but you also understand.

"Remember all this. When you master these, come back, and I will teach you the rest of the chakras."

I sit there learning all the charkas when...

Chapter 10

HOME

The ground begins to shake and move. I stand up to keep my balance and look toward the moving bushes where I once came from. Everything stops as the maze opens and men in blue-green uniforms come out in a line. A very young tall man in a very nice suit comes out. He is walking toward me and stops, bowing to me.

"It's been awhile, Princess Haven."

I just look at him with a weird look as if I don't recognize him.

"Haven, don't you remember me? I have changed a lot and look more handsome, right? Let me introduce myself again. I am Vlalore, future king to the witch and wizard world."

I look at him like, "Oh, you mean the perverted guy when we first meet, who also came in room while I was trying to dress." I see him blushing. "So, Vlalore, what are you doing here?"

He gets closer. "It's time for you to come home, your training is done, right?"

I nod my head yes. "So, soon-to-be princess, are you ready to go home? Your mother is eager to see you, it's been what, three years? By the looks of it, you don't look suited to meet your future husband."

I look at him with a confused look.

"Don't worry, I will explain on the way, but we can't waste time."

I nod my head okay. I look back to my master and bow to him as he bows to me. "Master, will I ever see you again?"

He just smiles. "Someday when the time is right, when all fails."
I wave bye to him. "Goodbye, Sachi, save us all."

It takes three days to get to the Enlightenment Kingdom. Vlalore has explained to me that the kingdom is in danger; they want to take my mother's rule away because she isn't married and it shows that our kingdom is weak, but Vlalore has told me that the evils want the kingdom for themselves, like what Mike, who came back looking for me, wants.

The elders are scared and have no other way but to marry me off to another strong kingdom to our blood kind and together as well as the gifted bloodline. I still need to get to the tree Mother talked about. My mother has seen Vlalore even though his mother forbids it. We are now at the kingdom gates. As soon as we go in, the streets are quiet; nobody is out.

I look around. This place was dead. It used to be so alive. I wonder what happened.

"Vlalore, why is it so quiet?"

He looks at me with a worried face. He sighs. "Your future husband decided to set a curfew and send everyone away to their house."

I look all around. "Who does he think he is? We aren't even married yet." I am filled with so much anger that I ride fast toward the gates.

Slowing down, I am about to say "Open the gates" when an arrow shoots right straight at my horse, piercing it in the chest. Angel falls to the ground, lying on top of me making me stuck. All of a sudden a strange man comes up to my horse, looks down, and stabs her in the heart; blood is falling out and all over me as I yell, "Nooooo!"

The man then looks at me. "You're next, peasant, get ready to face death." He brings his sword over his head and comes halfway down before an arrow hits his chest, knocking him backward, killing him.

I look at him as he gets off his horse, heading toward me in full speed. "Vlalore, why did you do that, you could get in trouble," I speak too soon, because the gates open, and there stands my mother and with a man next to her along with guards.

My mother run toward me. "Haven dear, are you okay?"

31

I am out from under my horse looking at Angel in shock. I say, "Vlalore."

My mother looks at me and then Vlalore. "Vlalore, you didn't, did you?"

He puts his head down.

My mother looks at him. "Vlalore, you know the punishment."

He shakes his head. "I know, tell my mother I love her."

We all stand up, and this man starts telling orders, "Take that man and hold him."

Soon his guards grab Vlalore and push him on his knees. A torturer comes up behind him with a whip.

"Mom, they can't do that to him, it's not right. Mom, stop them," I am pleading with tears falling.

The whip comes down. My mom tries to hold me back, but I break loose.

I run behind Vlalore and yell, "Stop."

The whip now is coming, hitting me in the face, knocking me out. As I fall, I can feel somebody catching me, holding on to me. I can hear voices.

"Do you know who she is? She is Haven, the future queen of this kingdom."

Soon darkness takes over.

Chapter 11

PRINCESS CORONATION

O pen, open, open. I try to open these heavy eyes; nothing is working, but I can see a light in distance. As I get closer, it starts to shine brighter and brighter until I am at the ancient city. I look around and hear a voice, "There you are, Haven, we've been looking for you." I turn around to find this man tall man with brown hair and blue eyes just like mine.

All of a sudden, others start appearing. "Who are you, people?" I look around until I recognize one, my father. "Father, what is going on here, and where am I?"

The blue-eyed man looks at me. "I am Edzax, and we are all your ancestors. We are here to tell you to set us free, you can break this curse, you have…"

Before he can finish, the darkness comes back, and I awake in my bed.

Looking around, I see Vlalore sleeping in the chair. I sit up and Sandra the maid walks in with a hot towel and warm water.

"Haven, how are you feeling?"

I look at her. "I am good, just sore. Sandra, what is that stuff for?"

She sets it down on the table next to my bed. "Haven, they are for your face." I am about to touch my face. "I wouldn't do that if I were you."

I look and see Vlalore getting up from his seat and coming my way. "Thank you, Sandra, you are dismissed." Sandra bows and winks at me.

He grabs the towel and places it on my face. I wince. "That was stupid of you to do, you could have died."

I look at him. "Well, do you think I was going to let them do that to you, no matter how much I like you?"

He stops and looks at me. "What did you say, so you do find me attractive?"

I start blushing. "No, I don't. I meant, no matter how much I—never mind."

He starts laugh. "Well, it's too bad, I am already taken in arrange marriage."

He keeps cleaning my face. I grab the towel from his hand. "Thank you, but I can do it myself."

He just stares at me, and then all of a sudden we kiss, but this kiss doesn't feel like any other kiss. Sparks are flying as we make out. But I have to stop. I think about my powers, Ajal and Vivi. I push him away, and he gets up.

"I am sorry, I shouldn't have. I better go."

He runs out there like a scared cat. I get up and go to a mirror and look at my face and see the mark; it's a little above my eyebrow and ends on my cheek like a deep cut. I get dressed to find my mom. I ask everybody on the way where she is; they say she is in the throne room. I head there, and when I get there, that same brown-haired man is there. My mother comes toward me and hugs me tight.

"Haven, I am glad you are okay." As we get done hugging, my mom motions the brown-headed guy toward us. "Haven, this is Duncan Serphent, he is from the kingdom to the north of us, the second most powerful in the gifted kingdom, he is your future husband."

I bow to him. "It's a pleasure to meet you, Prince Duncan."

My mother looks at us back and forth. "I will leave you two to some privacy, to get to know each other."

My mother and the others leave this throne room. I am left with Duncan.

"So Haven it is." I just nod my head. "I am going to set some rules for you, and listen carefully. When we are married, I am in charge, and you will obey by my rules."

That's when I turn around, looking straight at him with an angry look. "Look here, mister, you can't boss me around like some stupid puppy dog. I will have you know I am who I am, and you can't stop that. You won't, if you do, you will suffer the consequences. Do I make myself clear?" I turn on my heels, heading to the door.

"Oh, Haven dear, one more thing, stay away from that mutt you call Vlalore."

I ignore him and keep on going.

I head straight to my room when Sandra stops me. "Oh, Haven, you are needed in the ballroom." She bows, taking a leave.

I head straight toward the ballroom when I hear, "Oh, Haven, you going this way too?"

I shake my head at Vlalore. As we enter, I freeze midway; the details of the ballroom are so well put together I want to cry. Soon my eyes spot my mother, who is over in the corner talking to someone. I head her way. As I get closer, I realize that this person is no other than Avisha Chess, who also belongs to the witch and wizard kingdom. My wonderful mother soon turns around.

"Haven, you remember Princess Avisha? She helped you escape that evil spirit Mike."

I am hoping not to find him or that Jaffar guy again.

Soon Vlalore joins us. "So, Mother, why have you called all of us in the ballroom?"

My mother's face has a huge grin. "Well, Haven, since you are back, I think it's time you officially become the princess of the Enlightenment Kingdom."

That's when Vlalore speaks, "That actually sounds like a great idea."

Avisha just stays quiet when I speak, "So, Mom, when is this what do you call it?"

We all stare at my mother.

"It's called the princess coronation."

We say "Oh" at the same time.

"We will have it in three days."

Avisha's mother calls her as I am left there with my mother and Vlalore. I turn to my mother, who is over on the side play a musical ball dance.

"Come, Haven, you need to learn how to dance this. Vlalore can be your partner, now, now don't be shy. Put your hand on his shoulder and the other in his hand."

We do as Mother says, and he puts his hand on my waist and his hand with mine. He leads, and I follow. I look at our feet and keep messing up, and he laughs. Mother starts to pout.

"Haven, instead of looking at my feet, look at my eyes."

Mother starts the music all over again. I stare at his eyes like he says, and we dance.

This man's eyes are the greenest I have ever seen them; they are beautiful. When I look at them, I am lost. These are the eyes of my other half. This man I am dancing with today is my future. I can see it in his eyes. I am betrothed to another, but he is the one I am meant to be with, but yet my heart and my mind fight over what to choose. I do not know which to follow. The music has stopped, and we just stare at each other in the middle of the ballroom holding hands. You can hear an "Aww" from my mother; she gets closer as we move away from each other.

I can see her looking between us. "I see now, but how is that possible, they couldn't have not done that."

Looking toward my mother, she starts to frown and leaves us there. We both part our separate ways.

As the days go by, the day comes. I haven't see anyone for a while, my mother or Vlalore or anybody—just people I don't know help me prepare for the coronation.

Morning comes. The day has gone and then comes the evening. It is time for the event to begin. I can hear people talking while I await behind the curtains. Soon I hear someone speak loud and clear; that voice has to be Jaffar.

"Ladies and gentlemen, we are here today to crown a princess, so I welcome you, Haven Angel Enlightenment."

The curtains open, and there I stand in a beautiful long, wavy, blue dress. I hold my head high, walking to the front of the throne room, and I kneel down.

Then my mother steps forward. "Today marks a brand-new day, not only has your princess returned, but my daughter returns to the future. I, Egjyll Enlightenment, crown the princess of the Enlightenment Kingdom. All hail Princess Haven."

I stand and turn around, and everyone stands and says, "Hail, Princess Haven."

Soon the party comes, and I am to take the first dance with my so-called fiancée, who is nowhere to be found. Instead Vlalore takes his place. The music begins to play. I know if stare into his eyes, I can't stop myself, so I look away the whole time.

As the music stops, the door burst open. Five men walk in, along with five women and two others.

Chapter 12

SACHI

Everyone has stopped what they are doing and bows down to these people. My mother comes running up next to me.

"Haven, you need to bow. I will explain everything later."

I am about to do what my mother tells me to do, but an older man comes up to me along with the older women; they are both wearing different clothes from the others.

As they both come closer, my mother starts talking, "I am so sorry, Marsden Drachm and Cliona Carpathia." My mother bows to them, but Cliona talks, "It's okay, my dear, we know your daughter is new around here, we are so sorry that we are late." My mother nods her head like an okay. "We are the council of the witches and wizard, we are the ones that create the matchmaking for both the gifted and the witches and wizard."

I look at them all and bow somewhat. The woman named Cliona looks between me and Vlalore. All of a sudden she bows back, and whispers can be here and ahh's. The man, however, instead gives me a dirty look and walks away with rest of the council, but the women just stand there; their eyes are lock on Vlalore, who looks to be out of a daze also.

Cliona walks away to meet up with the rest of the council. The party goes on as usual. I step out to take a breather on the balcony. I look toward the sky. I wonder how my so-called other mom is doing.

"The sky is beautiful tonight, ain't it?" I look to my side to find Cliona there, looking at the sky; she then looks at me. "I know who you really are."

I am about to say something when she says, "Don't say anything, dear, just promise me that you will take care of my grandson. Save us all, blessed one."

She leaves me there in train of thought. Mom says if I need an answer to something, I can go to the library, and that's what I did. I search everywhere and everything on the blessed one.

"You won't find anything here on the blessed one, my dear." This is voice is creepy and deep. Out of the shadows a man comes out, but the man is no other than Marsden Drachm.

He walks out of the shadows and into the light. I looks at his eyes, and I see red all over.

"The blessed one is someone with the extreme power, and I know for certain it can't be you, you are too weak and yet to find your other half, I would have killed you if it wasn't for Cliona. You see, Haven, I know where your father is, your future, and your other half. You see, your destiny will soon be mine to control, all you have to do is give up your other half."

I look at him as he stands in front. "You call yourself a wizard—one, the head member of the council, and secondly, I don't even know who my other half is, so excuse me, sir." I head out the door and fast-walk to my room. When I get there, I go straight for a shower.

"Sandra, not now." When I get to my room, Sandra is there. I sit in the nice, hot bath. I wanted some quiet time to myself. I am thinking too much of what that man said. I close my eyes.

"Haven, Haven." I look around to find a big tree in the middle of nowhere; it is as tall as it could be. "Come find me, blessed one, you are the blessed one, come to me, you know where to find me." I awake still in the bathtub, which is now cold. I get out and change into some clothes and head for bed.

The sun shines bright this morning and brighter. I jump out of bed and head to the closet and change into some clothes. As I peek out the door, I look all around me; one is in sight. As I head toward the dinner, I walk past the throne room and hear a voice. As I am about to enter, Cliona comes out and takes me by the hand as soon as she sees me.

I follow her all the way to the garden and where a door hides.

"Haven, you need to leave and find the tree of life, they are looking for you, you need to go now."

I look at her. "I have to stay here, my mother is here."

She grabs me by the shoulders. "If you stay, there will be no hope for all of us or humanity, you are the blessed one, and your destiny is different from ours."

Chapter 13

THE TREE OF LIFE

Cliona pushes me through the magical door, and I find myself in another world, but this world is something I recognize somewhat. As I walk through this void, people just look at me, and then a woman who sees me walks toward me. I don't know where to turn to, so I just stand there.

"Haven, is that you, dear?"

I look up and find no other than my other mother Nina. As she gets closer, I say, "Mother, is that you?" I hug her, crying into her shirt. I can also feel her tears fall. I am so glad I've found her. The Lord only know what could have happened to her. As we finish our reunion, she leads me into a house and tells me to sit down.

"Mom, what is this place?" She looks back at me.

"It's the beginning of what could happen to all of us," she says as she sets down a cup of hot tea for me.

I pick it up, taking a sip from it. "Mom, so what actually happened here?"

She grabs her cup and sits with me. "Your birth mother, even though your father sacrificed himself for us, somehow this place was destroyed." She takes a sip. "So this place is where all the humans come or was already part of this world." She puts her cup down. "This place was were your mother once lived a happy life as a regular person until they took her away from me." I look at her with a weird look. "That's another for another time."

I place my cup down. "So, Mom, what do you know about the tree of life?" I say as she picks up my cup and her cup.

"I should just show you." She leads me through a forest, and as she stops, I bump into her. "Why did you stop?" I look at her eyes and where they meet. There it stands, in the middle of the forest, lifeless; nothing is moving or alive.

"Mom, what happened to it?"

She looks at me as I hit the floor with both my knees.

Tears start to fall. "The tree was my only hope, it's what kept me going. Why would this happen? I can feel it so sad and lifeless."

Mother goes to the ground with me and holds my face. "I am so sorry, Haven, please don't cry." She helps me up, and we walk away. As I take one step, I see the tree light up. I stop. "I will meet you back at the house."

She lets go of me and walks off toward the way we came from. I go up to the tree and say, "What happened to you?" I reach my hand and touch the tree, my palm lay flat, closing my eyes and breathing in. Energy flows from my palm into the tree. Images pop in mind of the future and present times, but the future is black.

I open my eyes and let go of the tree and stand back and just look at the tree; as it stares too, it comes to life as does everything else around it; the sun shines through the tree branches, and the wind blow and the tree is alive. The light from it shines brighter than any other. So I hear steps running my way. I turn to see my mother as she falls to her knees.

I turn back around to the tree, and soon a spirit comes out. As she walks the light follows behind her. She wears a robe of white; she was all white. She comes toward me, bows, and walks around me, looking form head to toe. "It's about time I meet you, blessed one." My mother is as if she were frozen. "Don't worry, she can't see me, only you can, blessed one."

I was about to ask her a question when she says, "Don't worry, I know, and I have the answers you seek. I am the tree of life, but we don't have much time, for this light will disappear, and only you can save us, follow, blessed one."

I follow the tree of life as she leads me through vines and vines of leaves hanging down, and there in the middle of the opening stands...the future?

She stops and opens a little path for us to get to the middle, and we sit.

"Now, Haven, I will answer all you seek. First, you are cursed and the savior of this world. The curse was placed on you by a wizard named Marsden Drachm, a head councilman who lived for too long. To break the curse you must find your other half and true love."

I look at her. "How am I supposed to do that?"

She puts her hand up and motions me to stop. "Haven dear, you already found him, the sparks are burning, but breaking the curse comes with a price. Humanity must disappear, and as the savior part, you must find that on your own, for I cannot help you with that. But once the curse breaks, all will be well, but humanity must disappear. It is our faith, you can't stop that."

I stand up. "What about my father?"

She tells me to sit. "As for your father, he is trapped by someone, use your skills and figure it out, control your death, love, life power. You can control it, you just have to believe in this."

She moves her hand, putting it over my chest. "Here is where you will find it."

I hear a bell ring and are back at the tree. She looks at me and walks toward the tree and turns back. Mother has been unfrozen, and I go to her.

I say, "Mom, let's go home," picking her up and walking away.

As Haven and her mom walk away, the spirit says one last thing: "A child will be born as the blessed one, this child's powers will be greater than any. The child must save us all from our destiny. The child will be born in the Enlightenment Kingdom, the child will be named. The future we see shall be for now until this child is born. As we come to terms of this mess this world has created for us, we must push back this madness and keep going forward. Until then, this world will have to wait for its savior. Haven, my dear child, save us all, for you are that child, please save us all. I will be waiting."

Chapter 14

THE TRUTH

As I and Mom get back to the house, there are three people there waiting for us—well, four people.

"Mother!" I yell running to her. "Mom, you are okay, I am glad." I turn around as my mother Nina stands there. I pull my mother Nina up to my birth mom, and they hug and cry. I just stand there looking at them with a weird look.

I look over and see Cliona and my future husband and him, Vlalore, Avisha Chess too. Cliona comes up to me first and speaks, "It's time you know the truth about everything." Both my mother look at me and nod.

"Yes, that's why we came here, Haven, it's time you know, we don't have much time left," my birth mother says.

We all walk inside Nina's house, and we all sit. I speak up, "So who wants to go first?"

That's when my birth mother looks at me. "I will, Haven. First, Nina is my sister little sister. I took on the horrible duty of the kingdom, it's a burden I bear being the oldest. Secondly, I had to let my only child go because of the curse our family bears, only the first born in our family bears the curse. Thirdly, your father is still alive, that's why we couldn't tell you about the tree of life. We paid a little price, and it caused so many people to go lifeless."

I get up and go to my mom, who is now standing by the window, looking out of it at the lifeless people. I hug her. "What do you mean lifeless?"

She turns around, looking at me. "Haven, these people used to have powers, and they used to smile, laugh. Nina lost her powers because of me, she was a great warrior in her time. Your father's city, which is now known as the lost city, lost its life, and dead, nothing can bring it back to life, they were the greatest ancient wizards of their time." She cries hard that Nina has to take her out of the room and into another.

Cliona stands and speaks. "It's my turn. I am your grandma, your father is my son, you have his eyes. It's my fault that he was gone. I told him to choose his own destiny, and he did. I have another son, you know him already, his name is Marsden Drachm, the other head, your father was supposed to take my place. I also was left in charge to match the blessed one with a powerful wizard."

That's when my future husband walks toward me. Cliona just looks at me and him and takes her leave toward my mother's room.

Vlalore and Avisha walk together toward me. "It's our turn. Avisha is my little sister, and I am the crown prince of the wizard and witch kingdom. We were sent by Master Sahib, who is also our dad and last wizard of the ancient city, to watch over the blessed one until she could fight on her own, which you can."

Avisha then leaves the room. Vlalore still stands there. "Haven, I… Never mind," he says as he walks away and then stops.

I am hoping he will tell me how he really feels about, but I know we can't be together.

He turns around and looks at me. "Haven, I like you. I am incomplete without you. I hate this guy being around you and touching you. I can't stand it, and I can't stand by and watch him next to you. I—"

I stop him before going forward. I need to hurt him; we can never be together. "Vlalore, we can never be together, not because of the curse, because you are a cruel man. I saw you kill those guys in the forest." I know he didn't, but I need to hurt him to protect him from myself. "I can't like a killer."

I can tell he is getting angry. All of a sudden his hand is on fire. Avisha comes in and takes him outside. I go to the kitchen to find my mother and my aunt and my grandma talking.

"Grandma."

She turns to me. "You are making me feel old."

I start to laugh. "Your son Marsden Drachm, what's his story?"

She turns and looks at me. "He is the eldest, and we have lived for years now, and well, the curse was placed by him because your ancestor Edzax took his love away even though my son never loved her. So he curses her family and descendants, he didn't know your father would follow their footstep sacrificing himself for the world."

I look at her like, and that's when I put everything together. He is Mike at the other world, and he is Jaffar. He has been watching me this whole time.

"Mom."

They all turn and look at me. "We know now, that's why we had to get you out of there."

I stand in front of all of them. "I have one more question. What is the blessed one?"

Cliona stands and walks toward me. "Haven dear, you are the only who possess great power, you are stronger than us, you were chosen, there was another blessed one before you, but that person has chosen you to lead us to a better life."

I turn, looking out the window. "Haven, you already see what it does, the curse, but there is this saying we have on the witch, wizard side. A child will be born as the Sachi. This child's powers will be greater than any. The child must save us all from our destiny. The child will be born in the Enlightenment Kingdom. The child will be named. The future we see shall be for now until this child is born. As we come to terms of this mess this world has created for us, we must push back this madness and keep going forward. Until then, this world will have to wait for its savior. Haven, this is talking about you. I was there when this was created, my duty was to watch over Sachi, you."

I turn, looking at all of them. "The only problem is, how do I break this curse and save the world at the same time? I am only one person, let alone a girl of age of twenty. I am too young for this. My brain hurts, I need to rest."

I take a leave, heading to a room upstairs and jumping on the bed. Is there any way to break the curse? All I hear is I could break this curse and this and that. I am so tried. I don't know if I cloud really do this. Maybe they chose wrong. I turn to the side and just let my mind drift off into darkness.

Chapter 15

LAST PART

*C*urse, *curse* is repeating all over in my head. The curse is, when a descendant of the Enlightenment Kingdom family member falls in love with a wizard or a witch, they must die in fourteen days, which is two weeks, to stop the earth and humanity from disappearing. There is no way to break this curse, but some have said there is, and yet no one has done it. Breaking the curse comes with a price: humanity must disappear, but the earth remains. I start thinking there is a way to break this curse, yet no one knows about it.

I jump from the bed and run downstairs to find them still sitting there.

"Mom, is there a book about the curse?"

She nods her head. "I gave it to your aunt a long time ago."

I look over at my aunt. "Do you have it?"

She gets up and walks, leaving the room, over to a bookshelf and brings it out. The golden plate covers shine like no other. She hands it to me as I sit on the sofa.

I flip the book over to its side and see a magical look. "Only the Sachi can open it." I look up at my aunt who sits across from me. "How do I open it?"

We sit there for a good hour until she remembers. "Put your hand over it."

I do as my aunt says, and the book opens. Flipping through, I find it, and just as I thought, there is a piece missing to the curse.

I go over to the kitchen with my aunt. "Look here, there is a piece of the curse missing." They all look away. "Oh, stop that, someone's been trying to stop you guys from breaking this curse, and why?"

They all look at the book, and I hear it close we all sit there in quietness. "There is one person who knows of the curse." We all look at my mother as she speaks. "Master Sahib."

That's when they both step in. "It's too dangerous for you, they are out there looking for you," Vlalore speaks, raising his voice loud.

I am always wondering why he would yell and worry about it, but it doesn't dawn on me.

"I will protect her." Duncan is standing right behind me as he says that.

Vlalore steps up and speaks, "I will lead you to where my father is."

Avisha soon comes into the room. "I am coming so I can control you, boys."

Mother stands up, walking toward us. "That settles it then, you guys leave first thing in the morning."

We all retire for the night, and as I lie there, a knock could be heard. "Who is it?" I get up and walk over to the door, hearing breathing.

"It is I, Vlalore."

I step away from the door and say, "Go away, I don't want to speak to you."

He turns the knob. "Please, Haven, I need to—"

Before he can finish, I hear a moan and see blood running underneath the door into my room. I open the door to see Vlalore on the ground, holding his side. Soon you can hear people screaming, and I can hear voices coming from down the hall. "She is that way, get her and bring her to me, now."

I act fast, pulling Vlalore in and trying to wake him as I whisper, "Vlalore, stay with me please."

I look around the room for a first aid, finding one under my bed. I take off his shirt, stopping, staring at his abs. His body is perfect.

"Like what you see?" He is now awake.

"Making jokes tells me you are okay."

He tries sitting up. As I start to wrap him up, the bleeding stops. I help him when the door starts banging. Someone is trying to break it down. I look over at the window. "Can you jump?"

He shakes his head no. "It hurts too much."

There is no other way out; the door is almost broken when, "Looking for me?" I turn around to find Master Sahib.

Vlalore looks up at him. "Dad."

Sahib comes over to us, holding us together; soon the door knocks down, and there stands Duncan with Marsden.

I stare at them and say, "You will never have the kingdom, they are my people, and I will destroy you, it's my destiny."

Master holds us tight as he teleports us from the house to the ground. He takes Vlalore into the forest. I turn around and look up to find them, looking out the window, and I say, "I will take back this world from you." I follow them as we hide. Voices can be heard in the distance. I just hope that my mother and grandma are okay and my aunt.

We walk farther in until we reach the tree. Vlalore looks at it. "It's dead, ain't it?"

I just nod my head yes. I look over at master Sahib, who is looking at the tree. "Master Sahib, Mom says you know the rest of the curse."

He turns and looks at me. "And what of it?" he says, looking at the lifeless tree.

"Well, what's the rest?"

We have walked in a complete circle, right back where Vlalore sits holding on to his wound.

Sahib sighs. "The last part of the curse is…"

Before he can say, it arrows are shot, and one of them hits him in the chest.

"Nooooo!" I yell, running to him.

"No, Haven, take my son now, you two are our last hope, go to the Rosewood Kingdom, and find a woman named Apollonia, she is the queen of us all. She lives in the Magical Kingdom where the statues meet, that's the entrance, go now."

I do as my master says and take Vlalore as we walk further in the forest. I keep walking nonstop. I am getting tired; we have been walking for days and days, weeks and weeks. Until I dropped all of a sudden. A winter storm comes in. I have dropped Vlalore on the side of me; my eyes start to drift away when I see a figure in the distance and voices as they get closer.

"Take them inside now, they must be cold."

I feel someone picking me up as they say, "Don't worry, Haven, we got you, you are safe now, all will be well when you wake up. Sleep well, my little sister, for I have found you."

My eyes close, and darkness takes over.

Chapter 16

THE TRUE ME

"*R*un, run, Haven, run, they are coming! Trust me, I must save you, Mother told me to save you. I love you, little sister, you are the chosen one of this world, and I, another. One day you will help me save the world, so that me and you may live in peace.*"

I wake up with a headache. I look around to find a tent blanks are thrown over me; that's when I think about Vlalore. I have to make sure he is okay. I head outside the tent and what I find was a beautiful place; it is winter, and the snow is as white as it could be. Kids are running with the wolves.

As I look around, there are about ten tents all around. I feel cold when all of a sudden I feel a heavy coat go over me.

"You might want to keep this on."

I turn I look at the person who has put a coat on me. This woman has a heavy brown coat on her long, wavy hair; it is a blue color, and her eyes are a blue and green, and she wear small looped earrings.

"Shall we talk then, and maybe then I can take you to him."

She leads me to a small opening area. I prepare myself in case she wants to attack me.

"Don't worry, sis, I won't attack you." She sits on a log covered with white snow. "So you must know about the curse that was set on us." I just nod. "Well, did you know that there is a piece missing?" I also nod yes. "Good. I know the last part to the curse."

I nod my head yes. "What is it?"

She gets closer and she says, "You," and she pushes me and starts laughing.

"Hey, what did you do that for?"

She gets up and says, "Remember."

All of a sudden flashes come back to me when I am a small child about six and they end.

"Follow me, sis." I follow her to a tree in the middle of the wintery forest. "This tree is called the tree of knowledge." She touches it, and she pulls my hand, and I touch my hand on the tree, and images pop in my head.

"Haven, come here, and look at this, ain't it cool?" She pushes me and starts laughing.

"Girls, come here," our mom calls us. She is all alone. And then an image turns into something cold and red. There they stand, the evils in this world. I try running, but I can't, that's when I see her.

"Don't worry, sis, everything will be all right, I will protect you."

The images stop, and I pull back, sitting on the ground as tears run down my face. The same woman comes over, wiping my tears away.

"Do you remember, sis?"

I nod my head and wipe the rest of my tears away. "What is your name?" As we stand she tells me her name.

"My name is Apollonia, your older sister."

I hug her. "I found you, Master Sahib told me to find you."

She laughs. "He is one good teacher, ain't he? Man, I miss him. How is he?"

I look at her and then put my head down, sighing. "He didn't make it. Mom got lost and Auntie did too as well as Grandma." I can feel her hugging me tight.

As we get down from hugging, we both walk back when all of a sudden I see Vlalore sitting down talking to other men.

"Go see him, he was worried about you more than his own wound."

I walk toward them. "Do you mind, gentlemen, if I sit here next to you, sir?"

Vlalore turns around and says, "Yes, miss, you can take a seat here." He turns back around and then freezes in place and then turns back around, jumping from his seat. "Haven, you're alive!" He hugs me tight, and all the men start to laugh and walk away, leaving me and Vlalore alone.

He motions for me to sit down. "Are you okay, and your wound?"

He says, "Don't worry about me, I am made from stone." We both laugh. I stop and say, "I am glad, I thought I lost you."

He looks at me. "You will never lose me."

I just smile at him. We both stand when my sister runs to us. "I need you both in my tent now." We follow my sister into her tent. She motions for us to sit; we do.

"So, sis, what is this about?"

She is pacing back and forth. "What are you guys doing here, anyways? This side of the world is blocked by a spell no one can get through. I was left here to take my place as the ruler of all because Mother couldn't handle this place, so she went back to the other side of the world to take her mother's place, and I wanted to tell you the rest of the curse."

I get up and say, "Oh, well, we pushed here, and when I fell, the winter storm came, and that's when I saw the two statues and you."

She thinks to herself. "You must have broken the barrier, you and Vlalore, why?" She stops in her tracks. "No, it can't be, the curse, the last part of the curse was, 'to break the curse, you must love your other half,' it makes sense now. Mom never loved her other half, and Dad didn't either, and our ancestors didn't. That would mean... Oh my."

We both look at my sister.

"You two are—"

Before she can finish, a soldier comes in. "My queen, it's them. They are here for you and your sister."

My sister stands up, giving orders to them, "Tell the villagers to leave at once." The soldier bows and takes off. "You two, come with me, we have things to do."

Chapter 17

ELEMENTAL KINGDOM

W e journey afar to faraway lands to finding solutions, in the nasty weather and beautiful ones.

"Apollonia, where are we headed?" I say, moving closer to her while climbing a green grass meadow. She just keeps on walking, not saying anything to me at all.

Soon we reach the top we climb for a while. I bump into her. "What is it?" I look to where her eyes meet, and there stands a tall castle about three stories high. It is the biggest I have ever seen, better than Mom's.

"What is this place?" Vlalore has caught up with us. "Welcome to the Elemental Kingdom, this is where we will help our first ruler, who is also a close friend of ours."

Loud noises can be heard in the distance as we duck behind bushes, making our way down. We see an army charging toward the castle.

"Haven, Vlalore, see those people charging toward the castle? That is no other than Queen Silva's men."

As we watch from afar, I get this weird feeling wanting to help them. "You feel it, don't you, sis?"

I just nod my head and look back at the scene before me.

Next, the soldiers retreat behind the forest as we wait for all of them to go back. We follow them back to their camp; as we enter, everyone is looking at us. Apollonia leads us to the biggest tent, and there in front stand two guards.

"What are you here for, peasant?"

They both block my sister's way as she stands up to them. Do you know who I am? You should move."

They both came closer to her. "You need to go away, half breed."

Apollonia soon takes a punch, but the dark-haired guard stops it and lifts Apollonia and throws her. Vlalore catches her in time.

It is my turn. "My sister said to move, big guy." They both start to laugh. "This tiny girl thinks she can boss us around." The dark-haired guy comes closer, bringing his fist down. I, of course, stop it and look at them smiling while his face is in shock, trying to get out of my grasp. I run up to the tree that is nearby holding on to his arm and twisting it and using all my strength, pulling him up and over me as I scream, "Aaaahhhhh!" He lands right in the dirt, unable to move.

That's when a woman comes out of the tent and looks at us. Her hair is brown, and her eyes are purple; she is wearing a war coat. She is now walking toward us but stops when she sees Apollonia and runs toward her. Everyone around us has stopped and looked at them.

"Are you okay? Who did this to you?" She looks at me and then the guy on the floor.

She turns her attention back to Apollonia. "Can you get up, my queen Apollonia?"

As soon as everybody hears that name, they all drop to their knees with their hand out, bowing to her. The guy I took down finally wakes up and bows to them as they pass.

"I am so sorry, Queen Silva." She just keeps walking toward the tent.

Vlalore and Apollonia enter, but before they can, Silvia comes back out, standing right in front of me, and says, "You, did you lay a finger on my queen or a hair? I will kill you myself. Do I make myself clear?" Before I can say anything, she walks back in, and Apollonia is sitting down, and Silva is giving me death stares.

My sister notices. "Silva, are you all right?" She shakes a no. "If this girl right here lays a finger on my queen, then I will."

My sister silences her, "Silva, this is my little sister, Haven."

She stops right in her tracks and bows lower than any other. "I am so sorry, I didn't know."

I go over to her and tell her, "It's all right, but I don't like when people bow to me, it's just not right to me."

She stands up and laughs. "Just like your sister."

Silvia looks back at Apollonia and says, "Anyways, my queen, what are you doing here anyways?"

"We are here because we are being chased, and he is coming for us finally, because of the curse we both bear."

I look at my sister with a confused look. "Wait, Apollonia, you have the curse too?"

She nods her head yes and sighs. "I think you need some education on things. Don't you know, Mom hasn't told you everything."

I just shake my head no. "First, Haven, do you know what you are?"

I nod my head yes. "Okay, you are the blessed one, who is the person who will save us all from our destiny as a world, but to do that, you must have the protector, he or she is also known as faith protector, and she has followers that protect her, in case the blessed one and the protector get separated. Good so far?"

I nod my head yes.

"Okay, now, if the blessed one is on her own, here other half comes along and protectors her until her real protector comes. Now you understand your part, right?"

I nod my head yes.

"Okay, now, the curse is spread among the siblings in some cases, which in our case we are, but Mom and her sister, only one took the burn, which doesn't make sense at all. Anyways, so we share the same faith but one of us must find our other half and love them, unfortunately for me, my other half is dead, he died in a war that took over my kingdom. Anyways others will come, but it won't be the same. But you, my sister, have found your other half, if you can't see who it is by now, then you are dumber than I think you are."

I just look down toward the ground, processing all this in my head. "So who is my protector?"

Everyone looks at Apollonia.

"I am the faith's protector, that's why we met where the worlds end, now why I am also here for was because the kingdom was taken by him, their true leader, who wants to destroy all the light and bring darkness to this world. His name, you know, sis, Marcus, also known as Marsden Drachm."

I stop in train of thought. "But aren't they dead?"

Apollonia gets up and walks out, opening the opening to the tent. "No, he is not dead. Edzax Enlightenment is also still alive as well as Hope Awakening, our ancestors are still alive, just stuck in time, like Father. There is the saying, I can't remember what it was."

I think to myself and remember it. "Sis, is it this one?"

> Time is...
> Too slow for those who wait,
> Too swift for those who fear,
> Too long for those who grieve,
> Too short for those who rejoice,
> But for those who love,
> Time is eternal.

My sister looks at me. "Yes, that's the one—they waited, feared, grieved, and rejoiced but didn't love, so they froze in time, but those who love time is eternal. That's means..." My sister sighs again. "I could well end up like them if we don't hurry, time is limited. Sis, you must find your other half and do what must be done, but remember, don't love a witch or wizard, or we are all doomed. Anyways, Silva, let's go get the Elemental Kingdom back."

We just follow Apollonia all the way to the battlefield.

"So what's the plan?" I say as we keep walking.

"There is no plan." We all stop in our tracks as Apollonia keeps going, summoning a sword in her hands, yelling "Come on, Marcus, I know it's you."

We all hide behind a bush, leaving my sister on her own for now.

Soon an army comes out. "She won't take them on, will she?" I say with worry in my voice.

Silva looks at me. "You need to get to know your sister, she is stronger than you think."

We watch as the army charges toward her; she stands in ready position, not moving. She is taking a stand.

Next, she brings her sword up and then down in one swipe; the army goes back, but it's not enough. They all come back and Apollonia is too weak.

"She won't make the last hit she took, she won't last long, she's too weak in her human form, we need to do something."

They all just sit there. They are closing in on her. I am getting so anxious. I want to do something. I can't help anybody that I love; that time when I was at home, I couldn't save my aunt from him. I couldn't save Avisha or Mom or even Vlalore. I am helpless. How am I supposed to save the world when I can't even protect myself? I am useless

"No, you are not, my daughter, you are stronger than that. It's time you use your true powers. Learn to control it and use it well, we will be watching."

I listen to the voice inside my head and close my eyes, putting my hands together in a triangle form. I focus on the chakras that I learned so far. I can feel them flowing through me as I sit there for a while, breathing in and out; everything around me goes quiet. Then I open my eyes and speed toward my sister.

Soon the army reaches her, and I jump in front of her and call out, "Ajal!"

Soon the Ajal army comes out and attacks the other army, and I make an Ajal circle around me and my sister. She looks at me.

"Haven, your eyes, your true eyes are showing, blue and red. Blue for Vivi and red for Ajal."

I look at her. "What do you know about my true powers?"

She turns and smiles at me. "Ajal is death, and Vivi is life that's why you are the blessed one, these two make you who you are, but

I know this isn't your full power, there is more to it, and if we live, I will teach you the rest of the charkas."

I just smile at her. I look back at the army I have made, and soon I am losing energy; I am becoming weak.

My sister comes next to me. "Haven, can you hold on a little longer? My human period is almost up."

I turn and look at her and nod yes. "I will try, sis." I close my eyes, putting my hands together and focus on my energy. I can feel myself get weaker and weaker. "Sis, I can't hold on much longer."

I let go, and that's when she says, "That good's, take a rest now, sis, I got the rest."

I sit down, watching as my sister takes over the rest. She uses her sword, and soon wings come out of her, and she flies bring enemies down with her from left to right; she is amazing. I can feel my eyes close. Soon darkness takes over.

Chapter 18

MY OTHER HALF

I wake up in some weird castle in a weird bed and room. I look to the door as the knob moves. I get up and stand in front of the door, ready to attack; when the door opens. I move my hand quick, going in for a punch when someone stops me. I look up, and there stands no other than Vlalore with my sister's hand on mine, stopping it.

"It's okay, Haven, you are safe now, no one is going to hurt you."

As my sister lets go, I put my hand down. I am ready to fall when Vlalore is there in seconds catching me. "You need to rest, love."

When did he start calling me that? My sister looks at us.

"If nobody is going to tell her, then I will. Haven, this is your other half, he is made for you."

I just stare at my sister. "That can't be, you're a wizard."

My sister looks at me. "That is weird, but do you every feel sparks when you two touch?"

My mind goes back to those time when we touched and kissed; they are all different. It is like I need him, wanting him next to me; he makes me worry. I look at Vlalore, who looks back at me.

"We can't be together, you're a wizard, and I can't be with a wizard, so, Vlalore, go back and marry that girl. I am sorry," I say this with my head down.

From the corner of my eye, I see him get up and storm out. Before he can shut the door, he says, "If that's what you want, then fine, so be it. I will leave then, bye forever, Haven." The door shuts, and it's me and my sister left.

"Well, that went well, sister, the curse says to break the curse, you must love your other half."

I look at my sister. "It also states that you can't fall in love with a wizard, so leave, I want to be alone."

I pull the cover over me and lie down when the cover is pulled off. "No, you have a world to save, come on. I said I would teach you the rest of the charkas if we lived, and we did."

I look at her with an angry face and then sigh. I get up and get dressed in some combat clothes. She leads me outside and on to this combat field.

"So let's see what you know so far, shall we? Hit me with your best shot."

I look at her in ready position. I just stand there, and she runs, but the next thing I know, her sword comes out and she swings it at me.

"Sis, are you crazy or trying to kill me?"

She stops and looks at me; her eyes turn to their color, blue and green "I will try not to. Just show me what you got."

I put my hands together and breathe, thinking and feeling the three charkas I know flowing through me. Everything goes quiet, and that's when I hear footsteps. She is running at me. I open my eyes. I feel them changing. I charge at her and see her smile; her sword comes down, and I summon something I could never do before, but it's a staff on fire.

As our weapons cling together, I look at her eyes, and I realize I am losing my strength, and she backs away.

"Haven, learn how to control your energy, but then again, you need to learn the other charkas."

I breathe and close my eyes, and I feel more energy coming to me, but where is it coming from? I look at her and charge toward her, and I throw my staff at her.

"You missed, where did you go?"

I can see her looking around her. I soon come right up behind her, kicking her with all my strength.

She lands right on her feet. "Not bad, sis, but that's enough. I will now teach you the rest of the charkas."

I stand up, making my staff disappear, almost falling on my knees as my energy is draining. "Be careful, rest for a moment, and I will just tell you."

I do as she says, sitting down in the grass area. She comes over to me and sits. "So let's begin, shall we? Now the fourth charka is the heart chakra—the wellspring of love, warmth, compassion, and joy—it is in the center of the chest at the heart level.

"Anahata moves love through your life. It is the center of your deep bonds with other beings, your sense of caring and compassion, your feelings of self-love, altruism, generosity, kindness, and respect. Anahata is an integrating and unifying chakra—bringing to wholeness—as such, it is your healing center. Indeed, most spiritual traditions recognize love as the ultimate healing force.

"The energy of Anahata allows us to recognize that we are part of something larger, that we are interconnected within an intricate web of relationships extending through life and the universe. Anahata allows us to recognize and get in touch with the sacred and fundamental truth that runs through all of life and connects everything together. The 'way of the heart,' or the 'path of the heart' is living your life from this energy center of love.

"It means living your life with loving kindness and compassion toward others. It means that your heart is open to others and you inspire kindness and compassion in others. You create a safe and supportive environment. Others can feel your love and warmth. They feel loved and accepted unconditionally. People feel at peace around you, as there is no judgment coming from you. When Anahata is open and energy is flowing freely, you are not only loving to others, you are also loving to yourself. You know when you need to say no and when you need care and self-nurturing.

"All the seven chakras are important, and while I cannot say that the heart chakra is the most important, I do want to say that it is very important. Most of the world's spiritual traditions recognize love as the unifying force, the energy that is the most fundamental part of the universe, and of ourselves. To be open to love is to reach to the deepest places and connect with our true essence, our spirit, and our soul.

"Now the fifth charka is the throat chakra, and it is the first of the higher or spiritual chakras on the 'chakra ladder.' This chakra is in the region of neck and shoulders, and its color is blue. The gift of this chakra is accepting your originality, expressing your authentic voice, and speaking your truth. The energy of this chakra allows you to seek knowledge that is true, beyond limitations of time and space, beyond cultural and family conditioning. The main challenge for the fifth chakra is doubt and negative thinking. When you gain and verify your knowledge through meditation and direct experience, then doubt and negativity are removed.

"The "way of the throat chakra" is the way of inspired creativity and seeking and sharing of the truth. It is the way of standing up for what you believe, saying no when you need to, and being open and honest in what you say. Do you dare to be creative? Do you dare to open to a life full of infinite possibilities? The fifth chakra is linked directly to your personal integrity and a sense of honor. As a communication center, it not only allows you to express who you are and what you stand for, but also allows you to listen deeply to another. A person with an open Visuddha chakra is a good listener, she enables another person to have the experience of being heard—one of the most profound human needs.

"He has already taught you the sixth charka. The seventh is the crown chakra, and it is at the top of the 'chakra ladder,' which starts from the root chakra that grounds us on the earth and progresses upward to the Sahasrara, which connects us with the universe and the divine source of creation.

"Sahasrara is located at the crown of the head. The gift of this chakra is experiencing unity and the selfless realization that everything is connected at a fundamental level. The energy of this chakra allows us to experience mystical oneness with everyone and everything in nature. There is no intellectual knowing at the level of seventh chakra, but there is serenity, joy, and deep peace about life. You have a sense of knowing that there is a deeper meaning of life and that there is an order that underlies all of existence.

"The 'way of the crown chakra' is the way of going beyond the limits of your own ego. It is the way of transcending the ego and knowing that all of creation is interconnected at a fundamental level—a level that some call the 'Akasha,' or 'zero point field,' or just 'the field.' This is the fundamental level of connection.

"According to Tantric philosophy, the seventh chakra is both a receiver and giver of energy and consciousness. It receives energy to sustain life, and it gives back the personal energy to unite with the collective pool of consciousness. It is the meeting point between finite (the body and the ego) and infinite (the universe and soul). It is the place where time and timelessness intersect and where death and eternal life meet. The thousand-petal chakra embraces an attitude of gratitude for one's life.

"When we realize that everything is interconnected and that we are part of the larger scheme of life, we begin to live with gratitude, faith, and trust, rather than filled with fear and anxiety. We are guided by the higher power, and we feel divinity from within and from without.

"The challenge of this chakra is to liberate the spirit—open to the divine—and at the same time stay firmly rooted deep in the ground. With all seven of the charkas, they help you control your true powers, Ajal and Vivi. Now, sis, master your powers so we can save this world from its destiny."

Chapter 19

SACRIFICE

Every day since my sister has told me about the rest of the charkas, I have been practicing on them harder and harder. My sister and Silvia have been working on a plan to take back the kingdoms, but I have a plan on my own. I am just deciding if I am going to include them in it. I look different. I look more fit and grown-up.

As I finish my training, a messenger comes up to me. "Ma'am, this is for you."

I take it from him, opening it. "Who is it from?" But by the time I ask, he is gone.

The letter read, "Come find me where the tree has died, for I shall be waiting for you, come alone if you want to see them alive."

If I told my sister this, she won't like this. I have to go by myself; she can't find out. I head upstairs to shower when I bump right into her.

"Haven, there's something I need to tell you, can we talk in your room?" I nodded my head yes.

We enter my room as soon, and as the door shuts, she speaks, "The day you were born, I went into the next room with Dad. He told me to do that chant, so now they are trapped in time because of me. My other half didn't die in the war. He sacrificed himself when he found out about my curse. The tree was my doing it, it is dead because of me, and I feel guilty. I should have waited for you."

66

She is about to cry, but she is making me feel bad. I have to tell her, but how? They will find out.

I look back at her. "Sis, there is somewhere I need to go, you know, to build up my strength, so I need to leave as soon as possible." As I am telling her this, I take out the note and put it in the dresser, noting to her to read it as soon as I leave. "I wish you could come, but I need to go alone. I hope to see you at the kingdom." That's the clue for her to come alone.

She looks at me. "I understand, take whatever you need. I love you, sis, be careful."

I nod my head yes.

I pack and set off toward the tree of life.

I get there to find one here yet, or are they here already. As I look around, I can feel them.

"Well, well, she did come alone, you're a stupide girl."

I turn around to find one other than Duncan Serphent, the guy I am supposed to marry.

"What do you want with me?" He starts to laugh. "Oh, these people are yours if you marry me and rule this kingdom with me."

Soon he makes my mom, aunt, master, grandma and Avisha appear. I look at them and then him.

"If you let them go, I will marry you on one condition. Take me to Vlalore."

He nods his head and lets go of them, and they run to me and hug me.

Mom hugs me tight. "Haven, you can't marry him, you have to marry Vlalore, he is your other half, you two can be together you're half witch and half gifted."

I look at Mom. "But the curse."

She grabs my face. "To break it is to love your other half."

I understand what my mom says, but Vlalore is my other half. I need him now than ever. I am the blessed one. I am Haven Rosewood.

"I know now, but I must do this. I have a plan." I looked at them. "Bye, family."

I walk toward Duncan, who is waiting for me. He takes my hand. We are disappearing in thin air as a little hole is left. I see Apollonia with them. I know they are safe now.

Duncan takes us to the Enlightenment Kingdom straight to the throne room.

"I got her, Dad."

I'm like, "Dad?"

And then he turns around—my worst enemy, my uncle, Marsden Drachm.

"Hello, my dear, you will marry my son and become queen of all."

I look at him. "That's disgusting, you are cruel and mean and a selfish person."

He just starts laughing and says, "As for your other half, he will watch you marry my son, they all will, which is why they are all here." Soon doors open, and they all start pouring in.

They look like if they are seeing a ghost, but that's when I see Vlalore, who runs up to me.

"Haven, I didn't know you were back, congratulations, I hope you have a good life." He then walks away.

I want to tell him I need him and this is all a trick, but nothing comes out of my mouth. Everyone has taken their seats, and the wedding begins. I need help. I need to get out of this spell.

It's no use. Maybe I should just give up. A voice suddenly pops in my head.

"Don't give up, my daughter, you need to save us, we are running out of time."

I close my eyes, focusing on my charkas, releasing them. That's when everything starts to change. I have released Vivi. The spell breaks; Vlalore looks at me, and he sees my eyes. I can feel more power. My uncle looks at me and his son.

"It can't be, son, run, it's almost time."

His son runs. That's when I see my family and my sister Apollonia.

"You're too late, Haven, it's time for you to end, this world is mine."

Chapter 20

THE END OF THE BEGINNING

My family has run over to me. "You guys need to go, this fight is mine alone."

Apollonia hugs me first. "See you in the next life, sis, stay strong."

She walks away with Avisha and Cilona. Mom is next to hug me. "Haven, I am so sorry."

I hug her tight. "Don't worry, Mom. I am strong, thanks to you."

She walks away crying with Master Sahib. Next comes Vlalore. "Haven, I love you, always have and always will."

I get over to him and kiss him. "I love you too, until the next life." He runs off toward the others.

The world begins to crumble, and it is just me and him, the evil one.

Buildings are falling, trees and plants are dying.

"Marsden Drachm, it ends here for the both of us."

He laughs. "If it may be."

I release all my charkas, and soon I can feel Ajal and Vivi become one. I feel wings come out of my back. I can feel a horn come out on one side, and one side is black and other white, for the true colors of Ajal and Vivi.

"So this is your true form and powers."

I run toward him and grab him by the neck. "And this is the true power of a mighty wizard, my father could have beaten you." I take my dark side and say these words, "Ajal, curse you to hell, begone, wizard, for you are no longer." I take my hand and make a mark on him, and soon Ajal takes him as he dies.

The world still crumbles. Cliona pops up. "Haven, control yourself."

I do as my grandma says. "Cliona, why everything still crumbling?"

She helps me up. "A sacrifice must be made by Vlalore." That's when I drop to the ground. "No, he must live." I start to hurt.

Cliona looks at me. "They are taking over your body, Ajal and Vivi."

I get up and look at her. "Take me in his place."

She looks at me. "But, Haven, the world needs you, we don't know what's going to happen to you."

I look at her. "Please, when I wake, I will restore this world, do it now, we are running out of time, do it now."

She nods her okay. She tells me what to say, "I, Haven Rosewood, the Sachi, give myself up for this world and break the curse so all may remain."

A light comes from the heavens, and a man speaks, "As you wish, my child."

I can feel a pull coming from my body; my soul is coming out, and my powers release. Ajal and Vivi are no longer mine to command. Soon the light goes away. I fall to the ground, breathing slower and slower. I see Cliona.

"You became a legend, and I will tell it to the world."

I feel myself slipping away, and soon darkness takes over me.

Haven has sacrificed herself for the world she loves so much. Haven hears one last thing before she drifts off into darkness, that same saying…

Time is...
Too slow for those who wait,
Too swift for those who fear,
Too long for those who grieve,
Too short for those who rejoice,
But for those who love,
Time is eternal.

ABOUT THE AUTHOR

Belinda Calderon was born in Chicago Heights, Illinois, and raised in Venus, Texas. She is twenty-four and lives in Venus with her mom, and she has three sisters. She has always dreamed about publishing her book since she was in seventh grade. On her free time, she loves to draw and spend time with her mom. She is currently working at the DFW Airport as Office Personelfor a company called Gate Serve. She is excited to start a new journey in her life.